RUBY'S SO RUDE!

Written by Judith Heneghan
Illustrated by Jack Hughes

WINDMILL BOOKS

New York

Published in 2016 by **Windmill Books**,
An Imprint of Rosen Publishing
29 East 21st Street, New York, NY 10010

Copyright © 2016 Windmill Books/Wayland

Commissioning Editor: Victoria Brooker
Design: Lisa Peacock and Alyssa Peacock

Library of Congress Cataloging-in-Publication Data

Heneghan, Judith.
Ruby's so rude! / by Judith Heneghan.
p. cm. — (Dragon school)
Includes index.
ISBN 978-1-4777-5609-6 (pbk.)
ISBN 978-1-4777-5608-9 (6 pack)
ISBN 978-1-4777-5532-7 (library binding)
1. Etiquette for children and teenagers — Juvenile fiction.
2. Dragons — Juvenile fiction. I. Heneghan, Judith, 1965-. II. Title.
PZ7.H437 Ru 2016
395.1—d23

Printed in the United States of America
CPSIA Compliance Information: Batch #WS15WM: For Further Information contact Windmill Books, New York, New York at 1-866-478-0556

CONTENTS

Ruby and her friends were going on a picnic.

They all felt excited about their day out in the forest. Sometimes, however, Ruby forgot her manners.

"Please can you pass me my backpack, Ruby?"
asked Jasmine.
"Get it yourself!" said Ruby, rudely.
She pushed past and took off into the sky.

"Hey, wait for us!" cried Brandon.
But Ruby wasn't listening.

The young dragons flew over the treetops.
"Wow!" said Noah, peering through
his binoculars. "What an amazing butterfly!"

"Where?" said Ruby. "Let me see!"
She reached forward and
grabbed the binoculars for herself.

"Don't be rude, Ruby," said Noah. "You should ask before you take something that isn't yours."

"Oh, who cares about that?"
said Ruby, flapping her wings.
"I do," sighed Noah, sadly.

11

The sun shone brightly through the trees.
Jasmine flew down to the ground.
She wanted to put on her new sun hat.

"I never wear a sun hat!" said Ruby.
"Sun hats are for babies."

"That's a rude thing to say," said Jasmine.
"I don't care," replied Ruby, sticking out her tongue.
Jasmine felt hurt, though. She put her sun hat away.

13

The dragons were beginning to feel hungry.
They looked for a place to have their picnic.
Then Brandon saw a shady spot on
the other side of a stream.

"Ooh look, stepping stones!" he said.
"Much more fun than flying!
Let's jump across them, one at a time!"

But Ruby didn't wait for Brandon to cross first.
She pushed him out of the way.
Brandon slipped and fell into the water.

"Why didn't you say 'excuse me'?" complained Brandon. "Now I'm all wet!" He felt annoyed. Ruby was SO rude!

Ruby, however, wasn't bothered.
"Last one across is a dragon dropping!"
she shouted, hopping over to the other side.
She sat down on a log underneath a tree.
"I'm starving!"

Before the others could catch up,
she opened her lunchbox and
took out a big cheesy rock burger.

YUMMY!

Ruby was too busy munching to see
the slithery snake above her head.
But the slithery snake saw Ruby's rock burger.

"Watch out, Ruby!" called Noah, as the snake
swung down, pushed her out of the way,
and snatched the rock burger right out of her hand.

21

Ruby looked up in surprise.
Now the snake was coiled back around
its branch, eating her lunch!

The snake didn't look very sorry. Instead it stuck out its tongue and dropped some cheesy crumbs on her head.

"You are SO RUDE!" yelled Ruby, feeling hurt and sad and annoyed all at the same time. "Now I've got nothing to eat! You should learn some manners!"

By this time, the other dragons
had caught up with Ruby.
They all stared up at the naughty snake.
Then Jasmine started giggling.

"What's so funny?" asked Ruby.
Then she realized that she'd been behaving just like
the snake! Soon, all four dragons were laughing.

"I'm sorry I've been so rude," she said. "I didn't mean to hurt anyone's feelings. From now on, I'm going to be really polite."

Suddenly, her tummy rumbled.
She peeked into Brandon's lunchbox.
It was full of lovely things to eat.

"Would you like to share some of my lunch?"
asked Brandon.
"Yes please," said Ruby, gratefully.
"Thank you very much."

Glossary

annoyed a little mad

binoculars a handheld device with two telescopes used to see far away

coil to curl around and around

complain to express unhappiness

flap to move up and down or back and forth

slithery sliding easily over the ground

starving very hungry

Index

Further Reading

Beaumont, Steve. *Drawing Dragons and Other Cold-blooded Creatures*. New York: PowerKids Press, 2011.

Espeland, Pamela and Elizabeth Verdick. *Dude, That's Rude! (Get Some Manners)*. Minneapolis, MN: Free Spirit Pub., 2007.

Websites

For web resources related to the subject of this book, go to: **www.windmillbooks.com/weblinks** and select this book's title.